HEY DUGGEE

THE BEST SCARECROW EVER

MEET DUGGEE.

He is a great big cuddly dog. Duggee is in charge of all the fun and adventures at the Clubhouse.

Would you like to meet Duggee's Squirrel Club?

NORRIE
is a kind
mouse.

BETTY
is a clever
octopus.

TAG
is a gentle
rhino.

ROLY
is a noisy
little hippo.

HAPPY
is a very happy
crocodile!

There is always something to do at Duggee's Clubhouse.
What will it be this time?

It is a lovely sunny day at the Clubhouse.
Duggee is very busy in the field.
But what is he doing?

"What are you doing, Duggee?"
asks Betty.

"Woof!" woofs Duggee, pointing to his pile of seeds.

"Woof woof!" woofs Duggee, pointing to the soil.

Duggee is planting corn!

Well, Squirrels, if you plant a corn seed in the ground . . .

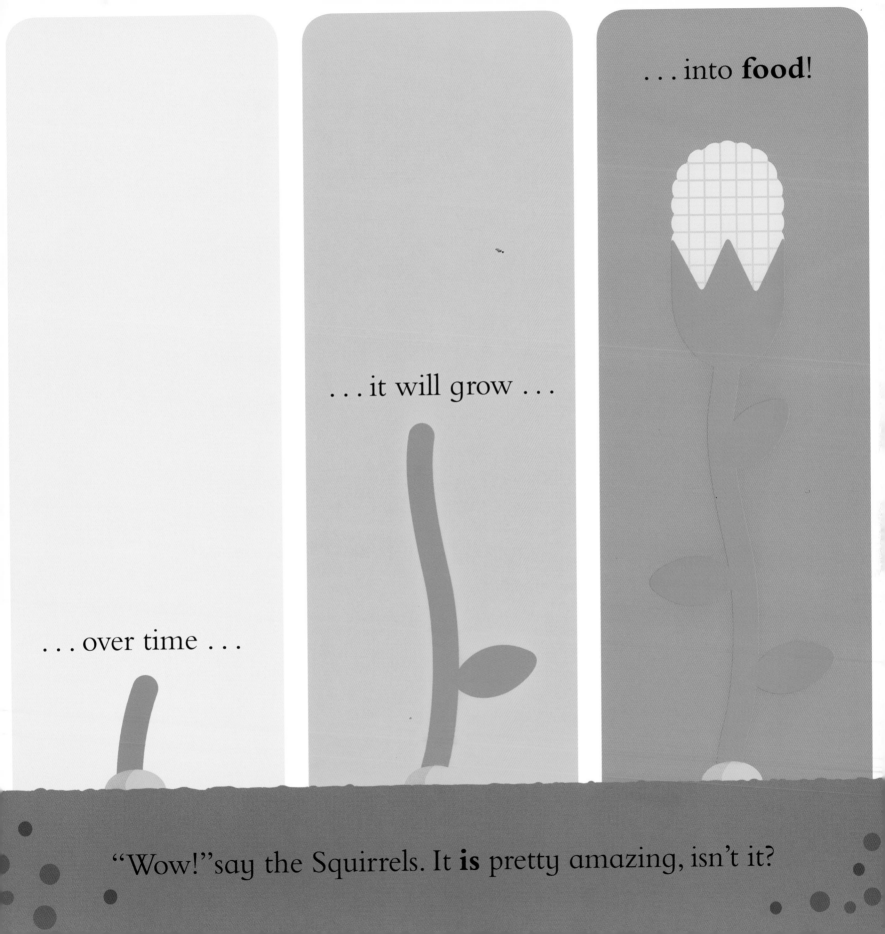

. . . over time . . .

. . . it will grow . . .

. . . into **food**!

"Wow!" say the Squirrels. It **is** pretty amazing, isn't it?

Oh no! Duggee is so busy planting seeds that he hasn't noticed someone has joined him. Someone hungry. **Someone who eats seeds!**

Duggee might not have noticed, but Roly has.

"BIRD!"

yells Roly in his **loudest** voice.

Roly's yell is so loud that
the bird quickly flies off.

CAW!

CAW!

"Roly!" says Norrie.
"You scared away the bird."

"Woof woof woof!" woofs Duggee.

It's OK to scare away
the birds if they're
trying to eat your corn.

But Duggee knows an
easier way to do it!

Because he has his SCARECROW BADGE.

You make a scarecrow . . .

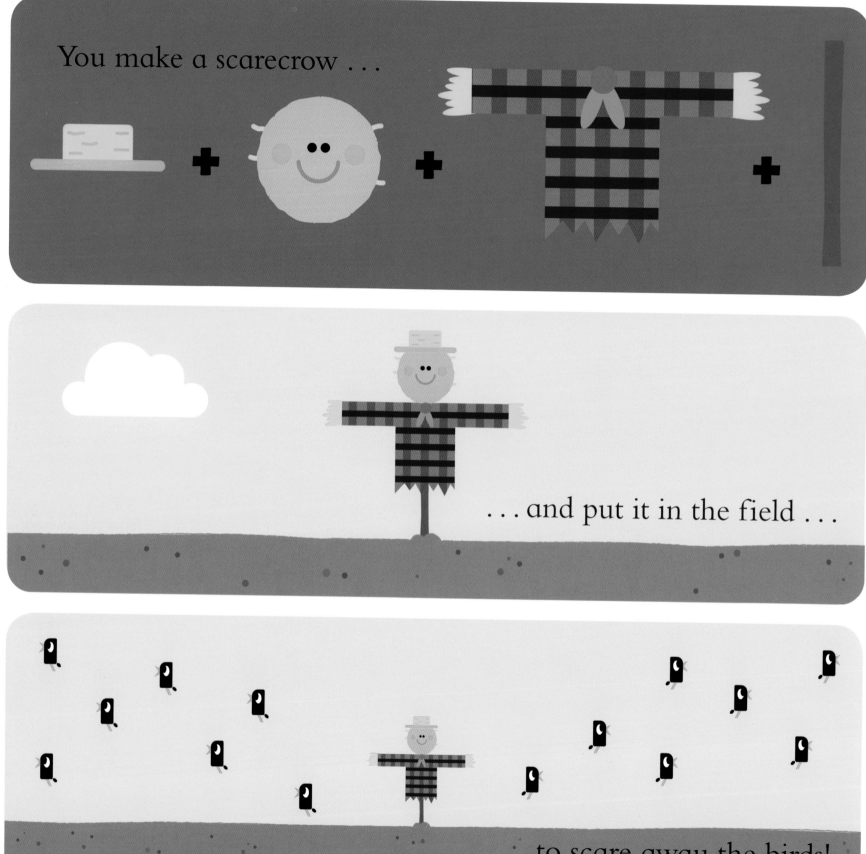

. . . and put it in the field . . .

. . . to scare away the birds!

"Can we make a scarecrow, Duggee?" asks Norrie.
"Woof!" woofs Duggee, nodding his head.
"Yay!" cheer the Squirrels.

They all hurry off to the Clubhouse . . . except for Roly,
who has decided to stay and keep an eye out for birds.

"What can we build the scarecrow
out of, Duggee?" asks Betty.
"Woof **WOOF!**" woofs Duggee.
Anything!

"Yay!" cheer the Squirrels.
And with that, they get started.

The other Squirrels are hard at work.

BANG!

CLATTER!

BANG!

"This is going to be **the best scarecrow ever!**" says Betty.

The birds are starting to feel hungry, so they have come up with a plan.

"WOW!"

They have hung a **massive** doughnut just out of Roly's reach. Roly, like all small hippos, absolutely **loves** doughnuts.

He can't take his eyes
off the doughnut!

Oh no! While Roly stares at the doughnut, the birds are pecking up all the corn!

Then, just in time . . .

. . . with a **crash** and
a **whizz** . . .

. . . and a great big puff
of smoke, out comes . . .

THE BEST
SCARECROW EVER!

CAW!

CAW!

All the birds fly away as fast as they can.
Well done, everyone! It worked!

The happy Squirrels run out of **the best scarecrow ever**, and join Roly.

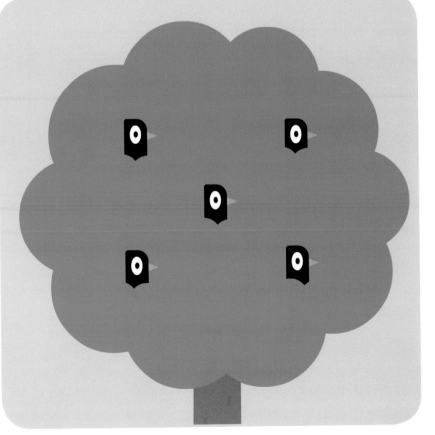

"The birds look really sad now," says Roly. "How can we cheer them up?" asks Norrie.

Duggee has a think.
"Hmmm," he thinks.

Aha! Duggee's got an
idea! What could it be?

BIRD

SCARECROW

CORN

Duggee disappears
into the Clubhouse.
He is busy drilling
and hammering.
Then . . .

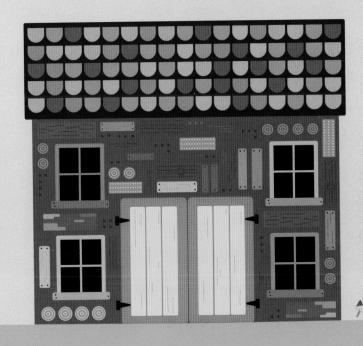

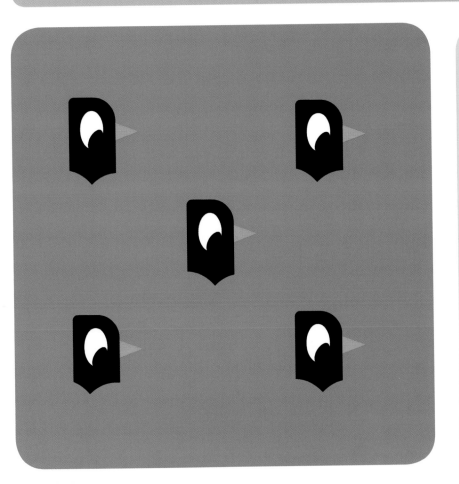

"BIRDS!"

calls Roly. "We made
you something!"

Oh, clever Duggee.
He's turned **the best
scarecrow ever** into **the
best birdhouse ever!**

"CAW!" say the birds. It sure is!

Well done, Squirrels! You've earned your . . .

SCARECROW BADGE!

"YAY!" cheer the Squirrels.

Now there's just time for one more
thing before the Squirrels go home . . .

"DUGGEE HUG!"

Can you earn your Scarecrow Badge? Do these activities, then write your name on the next page and ask an adult to help you cut it out.

Make the scariest face you can. Did it scare anyone?

What is your scariest NOISE?

Duggee was growing corn, a delicious vegetable. How many vegetables can you think of?

If you were going to build a birdhouse, what do you think the birds would like? Can you draw it?

Duggee said the Squirrels could build their scarecrow out of ANYTHING! What would you build a scarecrow out of?

earned their
SCARECROW BADGE